For Charlotte — my self adores your self.

With a special thank you to Mom, Tara and Daniel.

Tundra Books, an imprint of Tundra Book Group,
a division of Penguin Random House of Canada Limited

Library and Archives Canada Cataloguing in Publication

Title: My self, your self / written and illustrated by Esmé Shapiro.
Names: Shapiro, Esmé, 1992- author, illustrator.
Identifiers: Canadiana (print) 20210353031 | Canadiana (ebook) 2021035304X |
ISBN 9781774880234 (hardcover) | ISBN 9781774880241 (EPUB)
Classification: LCC PS8637.H3643 M92 2022 | DDC jC813/.6—dc23

Published simultaneously in the United States of America by Tundra Books of Northern New York,
an imprint of Tundra Book Group,
a division of Penguin Random House of Canada Limited

Library of Congress Control Number: 2021949353

Edited by Tara Walker with assistance from Margot Blankier
Designed by John Martz
The artwork in this book was drawn with pen, watercolor, digital elements and
countless pieces of buttered toast.
The text was hand lettered by Esmé Shapiro.

Printed in China

www.penguinrandomhouse.ca

1   2   3   4   5   26   25   24   23   22

Penguin
Random House
tundra | TUNDRA BOOKS

MY SELF, YOUR SELF

Esmé Shapiro

tundra

I have been
with my self
for a very long time.

MY self is not
YOUR self.

What is a self?

Is it INSIDE of us?

Or OUTSIDE of us?

Is it the way we feel?

Or how we make each other feel?

Is it the
things we do?

What we put on our toast?

The way
we button
our coats?

My self really likes your self.

I like the way you wiggle your nose...

and the way you TIP-TAP your tiny toes.

I like the way you bake
cranberry-butter-pie muffins...

and the way
you always make
enough to share.

Some say you bake
too much, but I say
there's no such thing!
(MOSTLY.)

I like the songs you
sing at bathtime...

"TWEE TWEE DEEDLE DEE
BEETLE BEETLE BUM BUM BEE!"

I like that whenever we
collect acorns, you always plant
one in the ground so it will grow
BIG and STRONG.

(Does an acorn have a self? I think so.)

I like that when we spot mushrooms,
I make mine RED
and you paint yours YELLOW.

I like that when you are scared,
you always sit on my head.

And when I am scared,
you always let me sit on yours.

My self is my very own self.

This is
my tummy.

These are
my boots.

And this is my
very special sprout hat.

I like that I always stop and smell the chestnut nettle roses.

You know what else my self
likes about my self?

I like that when my friend
is sad, I always have a
sprout they can
lean on.

And when my self needs
to be by myself, I know how
to be kind to my self.

I am never truly alone
because I always
have my self.

My self comes with me HERE...

it follows me THERE...

I bring my self EVERYWHERE!

My self is the
only self I have.

Your self is the
only self YOU have.

Your self is a lovely self,
so take some time to get to
know yourself.

You will see that your self
is a WONDERFUL self indeed!

And
side by side,
we can be
OURSELVES
together.